DAVY'S PIRATE SHIP ADVENTURE

written by Danual Berkley

illustrated by Amariah Rauscher

Printed in the United States of America by Danual Berkley

ISBN-10: 0692092188
ISBN-13: 978-0692092187

Library of Congress Control Number: 2018904019

The text of this book is set in 16 pt Bodoni font.
The illustrations in this book were created using watercolor and charcoal.

To Davion and Kai,

Don't ever let someone's misunderstanding change who you are.

Love,

Dad

Davy built a pirate ship to search the sea for gold,

But didn't notice he was followed by a monster on patrol.

This monster was the biggest monster Davy ever saw.

With big red eyes, and pointy teeth,

Davy stood and watched in awe.

The monster shouted, **"WHAT A FEAST!"**

And jumped into the air.

Little did the monster know, the kid was well prepared.

"SOMEONE MAN THE CANNON!" Davy shouted to his crew.

They pointed towards the monster,

And the cannon went

KABOOOOMMMMM!!!!

The cannon ball flew through the air,

And smack between the eyes,

That mean old monster blew to pieces,

GOODBYE,

GOODBYE,

GOOOOOODDDDBYEEEE!!

And so the search continued, Davy didn't miss a beat.

He made a few adjustments and the ship sailed towards the east.

But once again there was trouble, and a storm began to grow.

The sea began to spin and spin, and the wind began to blow.

And as the sea kept spinning it captured Davy and his ship.

"OH NO!" someone shouted, as the ship began to tip.

But little did that someone know, the kid just had to scream.

"PIRATE SHIP, PIRATE SHIP, BECOME A SUBMARINE!"

ZiP, ZiNG,

RiNG-A-TiNG,

FLiPPiTY, ZiPPTY, ZOP,

And just like that the pirate ship changed right there on the spot!

And once again the crew was saved, to search the sea another day.

Hooray to Davy who built the ship,

HOORAY, HOORAY, HOORAY!

And so the pirate submarine dove deep into the sea.

When they finally stumbled upon the gold,

They all had hoped to see.

Everyone screamed and shouted, "WE DID IT! WE FOUND GOLD!"

And that's the way the story went,

At least that's what I'm told.

Name: Davy
Age: 7 years old
Planet: Earth
Davy is Baby Kai's big brudder. He is a master builder, and spends most of his time building and creating new things.

Name: Baby Kai
Age: 2 years old
Planet: Earth
Baby Kai is Davy's little brother. He is the go-to person when Davy needs an extra hand. Baby Kai's favorite thing to drink is milk.

Name: Pip Squeak
Age: 31,511years old
Planet: Out of Sight
Pip Squeak is the guardian of planet Earth. Pip Squeak was sent to planet Earth after his big brother Space Kid Mike deemed it safe. He accompanies Davy and Baby Kai on their adventures to bring humor and good fortune. He has the power to give any Earthling magical abilities.

Name: Samantha

Age: Unknown

Planet: Earth

Samantha is Baby Kai's mother. She is also Davy's stepmother.
She is a master scientist, and problem solver.

Name: Danual

Age: 31years old

Planet: Earth

Danual is Davy and Baby Kai's father. He is a master of
imagination, and loves sweets.

Name: Teddy

Age: 4 years old

Planet: Earth

Teddy is Pip Squeak's mentor. Standing at only four feet tall, he's
extremely strong and powerful for his size. He was the first Earthling
who encountered Pip Squeak when he arrived on Earth. Pip Squeak
gave him the magical abilities to think, speak and walk like human
beings.